Banned

ANGEL DEVLIN

This book is a work of fiction. Names, characters, places and incidents are either the product of the author's imagination or are used fictitiously, and any resemblance to actual persons, living or dead, events or locales is entirely coincidental.

No part of this book may be reproduced or transmitted in any form or by any means, electronic or mechanical, including photocopying, recording or by any information storage and retrieval system without the written permission of the author, except for the use of brief quotations in a book review.

Copyright (c) 2017 by Angel Devlin

All rights reserved.
Cover by Lianne Cotton. Photo from Adobe Stock.

This book is dedicated to Tammy Clarke

Whose cover designs spark my writing mojo.

This book would not exist without you

CONTENTS

Chapter 1	1
Chapter 2	15
Chapter 3	27
Chapter 4	43
Chapter 5	49
Chapter 6	57
Chapter 7	67
Chapter 8	79
Chapter 9	89
About the Author	107
Also by Angel Devlin	109

CHAPTER One

STUPID RULES AND CALCULATIONS

July 2007

Evan

I'm supposed to be unpacking, but instead, I'm staring at the brunette in our next-door neighbours' garden. She's sitting on the back step with her head engrossed in a book. I'm engrossed in the fact that I can see down her top from up here at my bedroom window. We've been in the new house for a whole day now. I like that my bedroom's bigger than the one I had before. I do not like the fact that my father refuses to let me have my Xbox up here because he says I'll spend all day in my room. If I'm going to spend my time looking down this girl's top I'll be spending all day in my room anyway – if you get what I mean.

God, I'm starving. I hope my mum's been shopping. There's never enough food in this house, well nothing I want to eat anyway. She'll tell me to get an apple because I'm growing and need vitamins. What I need is a large number of burgers. Time to raid the fridge and cupboards to see if I can find anything that might fill me up.

I go to the kitchen and find my mum and dad having one of their boring conversations. I try to ignore them but then I hear the word neighbour.

"I'm aware you know her from school, Hazel, but don't encourage her too much or she'll be round all the time."

My mum has her hands on her hips so Dad needs to tread carefully. "Just because she's a single mother it doesn't mean she's desperate for friends, Jim."

"Yes, love, but we moved here for more room and to get away from bad neighbours, so let's just keep a healthy distance, alright?"

Interesting. My mum knows the brunette girl's mum from school. Surprised she can remember that far back. Joking. I love my mum, but hey, I'm fifteen, I need to act cool, okay? The best thing about this year so far is that I've grown six inches taller than her. She hates it when she's telling me off and I stand up straight and look down at her. Sometimes, when she's in a good mood, I stand and pat the top of her head for a laugh.

Of course, what actually happens, despite my dad's warnings, is that my mum and Sally next door become what they term — I'm going to puke — BFFs. Best friends forever. My dad ends up getting on well with Sally's partner, Adam, and they often all go out to the pub together on a Friday night. Both me and the brunette girl, who I discover is called Rachel, stay at our respective homes on our own. We're both only children. She's a year younger than me and fourteen.

"Can you take this parcel next door, Evan? The neighbours weren't in earlier but I've just seen Rachel go to the bin."

My body stiffens. "Can't you take it? I'm tired." I cannot go next door and face Rachel. I'll die.

"Don't be ridiculous, Evan. You've just spent twenty minutes in the back garden practising with your skateboard. You were perfectly all right then."

My shoulders sag. "That's why I'm tired."

"If you don't take it round I'm banning you from

your phone tonight and maybe all day tomorrow as well."

"God. Alright." I snatch the cube-shaped parcel from her hand.

It's always the same. 'I'll take your phone'. Blackmail. I can't wait until I live on my own and can do what I like.

I check my hair in the mirror. It's dark brown, shorter on the sides and longer on top, with a bit of a quiff I keep gelled in place. It seems okay in the three seconds I get to fix it. My mother rolls her eyes at me. "You're only taking a bloody parcel next door."

I close the door behind me with a little more force than is necessary and drag myself around to next door's front door.

I ring the doorbell.

Nothing.

I bang on the door.

Nothing.

I wait a couple of minutes but it seems she's not coming. Thank God. I can avoid the potential humiliation.

Just as I've turned away from the door I hear it open. Shit.

"Hey, Evan." It's Rachel's voice alright. Don't

know how to describe it other than it makes my stomach feel funny.

What I'm not expecting as I turn back, is her standing there rubbing her hair with a towel. Droplets of water have run down her neck onto her pale pink-orange coloured vest top. I can see her nipples through it.

"Evan? Is that parcel for us?"

I seem to have lost the use of my body. "Sorry, yeah, here." I want to leg it, but at the same time, I can't stop staring. *Eyes up, Evan, eyes up.*

"Sorry I was late to the door, I was washing my hair. Thanks for bringing this round. It's a CD. At least I think it is. They must have wrapped it in a lot of bubble wrap so it doesn't get damaged. That will be why it didn't fit through the letter box. Anyway, I can't wait to play it and then I'll be able to pop the bubble wrap. Bonus!"

"Right." I nod. "See you." I turn around.

"It's 'The Feeling'."

I turn back around. "What feeling?" I don't know what she's talking about but I can have another look at her now I've calmed down a bit. She's got nice lips and nice teeth, and freckles. Her ears are pierced. She's got silver studs in them.

"The Feeling. That's the name of the band. My CD." She waggles the parcel at me.

"Oh. Good. Well, enjoy it then." Evan. Stop! That's a conversation ender. "Erm, which one do you like best?"

"I don't really fancy any of them. I just like the words of the song."

I look blankly at her. What is she talking about?

"Oh. Did you mean which song did I like best? My favourite is *Fill my Little World*. Absolutely love it."

I stand there nodding. I can't think of anything else to say.

"Well, see you."

I go back home and throw myself down on my bed for five minutes, where I have a go at myself for acting so uncool.

Rachel

Diary entry from July 2007

The boy next door, Evan, is so hot. I'm naming him Heavenly Evan. He's got dark hair and reminds me of Harry from McFly. He came round to drop off a parcel and I told him about that song from The Feeling cos in class I made up a pop video for the song in my head, and in it, Evan realises I'm totally his perfect girlfriend. I'm not telling anyone I fancy him, even Tori, my bestie, because she might tell Mum. What am I talking about, she's the biggest gossip ever, of course she'd tell Mum, and Mum is friends with his Mum and she might tell him. So, it's my big secret, diary.

I'm going to do the math

E V A N H A L E

LOVES

R A C H E L A L I C E S U M M E R S

L's = 3

O's = 0

V's = 1

E's = 5

S's = 3

3 0 1 5 3

Add up to the numbers next to them.

3 1 6 7

Then 4 7 1 3

God, this takes forever. I should do it in maths class instead of thinking of my pop video.

1 1 8 4

2 9 1 2

This better be fucking worth it. I'm missing One Tree Hill *for this.*

1 1 1 0 3

2 2 1 3

I've had Rihanna's Umbrella *play four times now.*

*Oh, I can't be arsed. Our love is obviously **infinite**. **Infinite**!*

Or I'm crap at maths.

Ahhhh. Just like in maths, I've decided to us a calculator to help. The love calculator!

I typed in Rachel Alice Summers and Evan Hale.

77%!!!! That's fantastic. Well, in the nineties would be better but 77% means more than a three-quarter chance of things working out.

Maybe he has a middle name for better results?

Evan

Oh my God, oh my God, oh my God.

Oh my God, oh my God, oh my God.

I can never show my face again. EVER.

Or anything else. I'm scarred for life. I want to stay in my room forever, except I can't or she'll think I'm...

Oh my God, oh my God, oh my God.

I need to rewind time. Superman can do it. Why can't I?

Earlier this afternoon my mum barged into *my room*. She totally forgot her own rule, that she would knock on the door before entering.

She walked in, and I was looking out of the window at Rachel.

I had my hand down my shorts.

I wasn't actually wanking when she came in. I'd been about to though.

She walked in and I froze like an ice pop. Well, actually, it was like I froze with an ice pop, a large one down my shorts.

My mum looked at the general direction of where my hand was *resting* and got a bit flustered, dropped my freshly laundered washing and ironing onto my bed and rushed from the room shouting sorry.

I threw the clothes onto the floor and then threw myself face down on the bed, my cheeks burning and my knob most definitely no longer hard. I don't think it'll get hard ever again now.

But that wasn't the most mortifying experience. Oh no.

I'm downstairs now, and I need the ground to

swallow me up because the most mortifying experience ever is happening. My mother likes to talk about everything. She wants us to be honest and open and to have no secrets. I think she's scared I'm going to get a heroin addiction if she doesn't check in with me regularly and talk about every single subject that could lead to my early death or prison.

"So, I must apologise to you, Evan, for not knocking on your door before I came in. I had a chat with your dad earlier and we agreed it's time to put a lock on your door so you can have some privacy."

"Muuuum," I groan.

"Evan, it's perfectly normal behaviour for a teenage boy. You'll not stop you know? It doesn't wear off. Your dad still does it."

"Oh my God, Mum. STOP. NOW."

"Oh dear, I'm trying to apologise and making it worse."

"Apology accepted. A lock would be good. Not for *that* reason, but so I can keep you all out all the time."

My mum sighs.

"Now, Evan. I expect you to take your laundry upstairs when it's done. It's been on the conservatory sofa for five days which is why I'd brought it upstairs. I was sick of seeing it."

"Yes, Mum."

"Also..."

I tilt my head. "What? What have I done wrong now?"

"Rachel. You know, Rachel next door."

"Oh, that idiot." I apologised in my head for dissing her. "What about her?"

"I noticed she was outside when you, er..."

"Was she?" I shake my head. "I didn't see her."

"Well, anyway. I just wanted to make it clear to you, that Rachel is off-limits. I don't want to interfere in who you date, but basically, you can ask out any girls you like but not Rachel."

"Ugghh. I don't fancy Rachel. Yuk, Mum."

"Oh, well that's good. Because she lives next door."

"Duh."

"Don't be cheeky, Evan." My father tells me off.

I close my mouth and sigh.

"And, as you know we're good friends with Sally and Adam. I wouldn't want anything turning sour because you two decided to go out for two weeks and then have a major falling out. Or you get her pregnant or something."

I put my head in my hands. Maybe if I hide

underneath my fingers she'll go away and this conversation will end.

"Oh, that reminds me. Here." She taps on my hands so I raise my head to look at her again. "I went out this afternoon and bought you some condoms, because you're obviously getting to that age."

I feel my cheeks burn. Like I might need a fire extinguisher burn. Please, God, if you are there, just kill me now. "I'm not having sex, Mum. Christ."

"Well, you might want to soon, so just in case, here are a couple of packets. Keep a couple of condoms in your wallet and the rest in your room. A baby at this age would ruin your life, Evan. You don't want to be tied down and some girls around your age...Well, they don't want to work so they try and find lads to use to get pregnant."

"Can I go now?" I ask, mortified and ready to kill myself.

"Yes." She nods. Then she picks up the packets of condoms and hands them to me.

"I'll get your dad to fit the lock tonight. I'll send him to B&Q in a minute."

My dad winks at me. "Yep, and I'll make sure to knock before I open the door to fit it."

I walk out of the room at a brisk pace and climb the stairs to my room. God, I don't even want to spend time in here now, cos my mother will think I'm beating off all the time. I stare out of the window. Rachel is in the back garden again. She must love it outdoors.

She peers up and catches me at the window, and raises her hand in a wave.

I back away in shock. Now I can't even spy out of the window.

Can't spy.

Can't wank.

Can't date Rachel. Like EVER.

Life sucks. I might as well do my bloody homework because my whole life SUCKS.

CHAPTER Two

PROPOSALS AREN'T A MIXER WITH ALCOHOL

March 2017

Rachel

"Oh my God, his dick is huge and he knows just what to do with it."

This is what I have to put up with hearing all the time. Constant chatter about Evan Hale's monster member. I want to tell the women crowded around the bar to sod off, but Dan, the landlord, wouldn't appreciate it. I've worked at the Nag's Head for six years now. It started off as a temporary job while I went to college but I enjoyed it, so I stayed. Can't say I've ever had any high career aspirations. The bar isn't far from home which is another bonus. Yes, I'm twenty-five and still living with my mother and her husband, Adam. I receive many, many hints about getting my own place and they're ecstatic that I spend half the week staying at my boyfriend, Callum's, house.

I've been dating Callum for almost a year now. So, he's about to get dumped. Sorry, did you not hear that? Almost a year and bye bye, boyfriend. He's a great guy, with a good job. He's good looking, okay in bed. He's just...he's not Evan Hale.

I know, I know, I know.

Yes, I'm wasting my time and my life but I still have a goddamn crush on the manslut. Believe me, I have tried everything possible to get rid of it. He moved out of his parents' house when he was eighteen and you'd think that would have been the end of it, but no. I used to hang around my bedroom window like a sad loser on a Sunday to catch the 3.2 seconds of him walking up the path and into his parents' house for lunch. Then once I got the job here, I saw him quite a few nights of the week and every weekend. Always at a distance though. He'd always walk to the opposite end of the bar from where I was to get served, so I soon got the message not to bother.

I don't know what I ever did to him.

My sensible side knows he's a complete tosser. No, that's a lie. I don't have a sensible side.

Regrettably however, although he avoids me, he does not avoid other women.

Not in the slightest.

So, more often than not, I find myself standing here in between serving, overhearing some poor bitch's tale of woe as she pours out to her friends how the best shag ever went south.

Take tonight for example, it's just more of the same.

"So, what happened next?" Her best friend is eager to hear but has a narrowed eye. I can see she wishes it went bad for her friend. How charming.

"So, it was all over and I thought, god, I can't wait for him to wrap me up in those fine arms, and he said, 'the bathroom's downstairs. Let me know when you're done and I'll call you a cab'."

I snort and disguise it with a cough, then serve a bloke at the bar while still listening in.

Evan's shags are like a carefully rehearsed military operation.

- Seduce.
- Shag.
- Send out on their arse.

He never veers from his plan and there's one major rule that he never, EVER, breaks.

No one gets to stay the night.

What amazes me is none of these women are ever pissed off with him. They hunger for more, giving him doe eyes when he walks into the bar and perform resting-bitch-faces in the direction of the next object of his affection.

I really, really should hate him. The bloke is a twat.

Instead, what I want to know is, why has it never been me?

He's punched above my weight and he's punched far below it. Skin colour, hair colour, body shape and size - you name it, he's nailed it.

I'm probably the only person in Waterthorpe who hasn't bonked the Heavenly Evan. Yep, my teenage nickname for him became the name his conquests call him. Because they reckon that's what the experience is like — heavenly.

"Erm, can I have my pint then, love?"

I realise the pint has been overflowing while I've been eavesdropping and daydreaming. I make up some crap about it being a new barrel and running the beer through the system.

After the bloke moves away, I spot *his* dark hair, and watch his dark chocolate brown eyes fix on Anna, the other barmaid. He gives her a cheeky smirk that crinkles the sides of his eyes, and I watch her flirt back.

My next customer wants a packet of cheese and onion crisps, the box of which is, unfortunately, positioned right behind Anna. I move across and as I reach into the box I hear him tell her, "You're too gorgeous to be trapped behind a bar on a Saturday night." I can't help myself. I make a barfing sound while I'm digging in the box and then look entirely innocent as I get back up and give my customer his crisps. I can feel Evan's eyes burning through me but he can do one. He ignores me, so I'm not giving *him* the time of day.

As it gets near closing time, Dan tells me he's doing an afterbar with a few customers and asks if I want to stay.

"Thanks, but Callum is picking me up."

Not two minutes after I say the words, Callum comes through the door. His short blonde hair is gelled up on top and he's wearing a smart white shirt and black suit pants. He's a bit overdressed for the Nag's Head. He saunters straight over to the bar, leans over and kisses me on the mouth. "Hiya, gorgeous."

I hear a quiet but unmistakable barfing noise coming from a certain man's direction. Callum remains oblivious.

On my tiptoes, I lean over again, wrap my arms around Callum's neck and give him a massive snog.

"Have you finished work?" Callum asks, "because I want to give you your anniversary present."

"It's not until tomorrow," I say, my forehead creasing. I don't want him to give me a present, I'm going to dump him later. I can't have anyone getting too serious with me. I don't want anniversaries. I should have finished with him last month but he has a really comfy bed.

"I can't wait." Callum beams. "I had it all planned out for tomorrow, but nope, I can't bloody wait. Come around the bar, Rach."

"I can't. I need to clear up," I tell him, because I don't like the expression on his face.

"Nah, Rachel, you're fine. Take off," says Dan.

Trust me to have a nice boss. Why couldn't he be a slave driver?

I sigh, go around the back to grab my belongings and come out on the customer side of the bar, to find Callum on one knee.

Yes, this is how I dreamed of being proposed to. The groom-to-be on his knees in spilled beer and dirty footprints in the middle of a thronged bar on a Saturday night, with drunk people singing and half-shagging around the place and no doubt a pile of vomit somewhere nearby. It's a fairy tale come to life.

"Rachel Summers, would you do me the honour of becoming my wife?"

I look at the sea of faces around me. Although I want to break up with him, I can't do it now, here. Not in front of hundreds of people. It would be too embarrassing. I'll do it outside. Shit, he's put me in a right spot. I nod my head and mumble yes.

The drunks roar their congratulations. Callum puts what he tells me is his grandmother's engagement ring on my finger. It's too big and swirls around, but I say it's fine and ask if we can leave.

"Yes, let's go and find somewhere to celebrate, like in bed," Callum says.

I walk outside and get in Callum's car.

"Don't set off yet," I tell him. I turn to face him. "Callum, you're wonderful, but..."

"Shit," he says. "Shit, shit, shit."

"I felt pressured in there, in front of everyone. I'm sorry. I don't want to marry you. To be honest, I want us to split up. I took all my stuff from your house yesterday. Did you not notice?"

Callum shakes his head. "My mother called round. I thought she'd tidied up. But, Rach, I love you. Don't do this to us, please?"

"I'm so sorry." I remove the ring and grab hold of his hand, turning his palm up. I place the ring back inside it. "I don't feel the same. I wish I did, but I just don't. You deserve someone who will love you so much it hurts and who'll rejoice when you propose."

I jump out of the car and walk off down the street.

He follows me in the car and winds down the passenger window. "At least let me drop you home."

"No. It's okay." I shake my head. "I want to walk, it's not far. I need the fresh air."

With that, I watch as Callum drives out of my life. I feel guilty as fuck. The man loved me enough to propose with an antique ring. What the hell is wrong with me? I need to get over this stupid crush on the manslut. It's affecting my whole life.

Spotting the current answer to my problems, I walk into the off-licence and buy a small bottle of whiskey with a screw top and then I walk around the back of the pub and sit on a swing in the kids' play area. I know Dan's doing afterbar but I don't feel like joining them in person behind the bar. I am, however, going to join them in spirits.

The whiskey burns my throat. It's such a good feeling. Remarkable liquor. I carry on drinking and as I begin to mellow, I start to play on the swing and slides. After totally losing track of time, I hear patrons start to leave the pub.

"Party's over, Rach," I say, and then scold myself. "Sshh. Wait til they're all gone before you go home. Esssppeccciiallly if fuckface is with a bird."

As I get up and everything spins, I thank the Lord that my bar uniform consists of jeans, a tee-shirt and trainers, so I don't have heels to contend with, like most Saturday night drunks. Anyway, I'm just merry.

I sneak up to the side of the pub and peer around the corner to see if the coast is clear, only as I tilt my head, the whole pub goes with it. I fall arse over tit onto the ground.

"Rachel?" A dark haired, sex god looms over me, but not in a going to shag me way.

"That's my name, don't wear it out," I sing-song.

His face doesn't look happy from this angle, and where's his lay for tonight? He's on his own.

"Where's your Saturday shag?" I shout up.

"Pardon?"

"You know." I twirl my hand up from my position on the floor. Actually, I might sleep here. I feel a bit tired, plus the stars look so pretty in the sky. I sigh, content.

Evan plonks himself next to me on the ground. "I can't fucking stay in that upside down position, gonna be sick if I do."

"Seduce. Shag. Send home," I shout out.

"Are you drunk?"

I look around for my bottle of whiskey. Shit, I left it on the top of the slide. I sit up but everything spins around again. "Whoa." I put my hand up towards Evan. "Just give me a minute." The spinning stops and I get up. "I'm going down there to get my whiskey," I tell him.

He gets up. "You're not going down there on your own. You might fall again." Then he hiccups.

"Are you drunk, Evan, too? Is that why you've not pulled, cos you're so drunk it won't work?" I hold up my index finger and demonstrate it flopping.

"Where's Callum?" Evan snaps. "Why has he left you alone in this state?"

I stagger down the back of the pub towards the

slide. "Callum went home." I pick up my whiskey. "And I went to the offy."

"Fuck, Rach, I'm pissed myself. That must be why you're making no sense tonight. Why aren't you with your *fiancé*?" He spits the word out. "Wait until I see him, leaving you in this state."

"He's not my fiancé." I take another swig of whiskey and pass it to Evan. "Drinky?"

"You accepted his proposal, Rachel. That's usually what you call your husband-to-be."

"Yes, but then we came outside, I unaccepted it."

"You did what?"

"I unaccepted it. I took my yes back." I put my fingers and thumb together and make a pinching expression as if I'm retracting something."

"You said no?"

"Yup."

"But why?"

"Because he's not my number one. He's not my one. He's my number, er, maybe two. He's a poo." I cackle with laughter.

"You're *one* what?"

"I..." I sway a little as I make my speech. Then I poke him hard in the chest with my index finger. "I... am seduce, shag, stay the whole fucking night."

"I do not want to talk about your sex life, Rachel."

He doesn't get to say anything else as I launch myself at him, locking my lips on his and knocking him back onto the soft play area matting, the bottle of whiskey sails out of his hand and into some bushes down the bottom of the beer garden.

CHAPTER Three

LOSS OF CONTROL AND ALL COMMON SENSE

Evan

She's not engaged.

My inebriated brain hears those words and blocks out every ounce of common sense from my mind.

She's not committed herself to that wanker.

She's free.

No, she's not, my brain and cock command. She's *mine*.

So instead of moving her to arm's length when she launches herself at me, I try to cushion her fall, and it's me who falls with a mighty whoop onto the play matting. Good job I'm pissed. You bounce when pissed. All I can focus on is that Rachel is lying on top of me. Her dark hair is tickling my face. I grasp it in my hands, feeling the silken strands. They are just how I've imagined them on the too-many-times-to-count occasions I've jacked myself off in a Rachel fantasy. Then I pull her face down to mine and force her mouth open with my tongue before tangling it with her own.

I groan as my cock strains against my jeans. I swear it's going to punch a hole at the side of my zip. If cocks could sing and dance we'd be on stage winning Britain's Got Talent right now.

Then I hear a voice. "Really? In the children's play area? Up you get and off you go home."

We roll off each other to see Dan, the landlord, standing there, arms folded. "I have to say, I don't usually find my newly-engaged bar staff rolling around with men who aren't their fiancé around the back on my clear up."

Rachel sits up and looks at Dan with a fake look of guilt, but there's a tell-tale smirk at the corner of her mouth.

"I only accepted in the pub. I ditched him outside."

Dan shakes his head, a look of amusement in his eyes. "Well, thank goodness for that, because I didn't think he was the one for you. It's about time you two" – He points from one of us to the other – "stopped eye-fucking each other and got it on once and for all. However, you aren't doing it here, so run along."

We get up and I grab Rachel's hand before she can change her mind and run away from me.

Don't do this. It's a tiny whisper in my drunken mind.

FUCKING YES. LET'S BONE HER. My cock screams.

Guess which one I listen to?

Rachel

He holds my hand and we practically sprint to his house. That is, between stopping in shop doorways to snog.

He opens the door and that's it. My feet are over the threshold.

I'm in, right where I've always hoped to be. Where I've dreamt of being so many times. I wonder how my fantasy will compare to reality?

I'm in Evan's house. Fuck looking at the furnishings, Rachel. Where's the goddamn bedroom? Oh, okay, it would appear I'm being dragged upstairs towards it.

Whoop! I'm not actually sure if that's my brain or vagina rejoicing. Maybe it's both? "Whoop."

Evan looks at me strangely and I realise I did that out loud. Oh well.

At the top of the stairs there's a full-length mirror and as I walk past it I high five the reflection of my own hand. *You've done it biatch. You're through the door and upstairs. Go, Rachel, go!*

We're through to his room. It smells of his aftershave. His bed is dressed with clean bedding. The duvet has grey and black stripes and matching pillowcases. I'll bet any amount of money there are condoms in the top drawer of his wooden bedside table. This is how his stage is set out for his shagging show. I don't care who has gone before, just that I'm here now.

I pull my tee over my head, revealing a black lacy bra. Balconette style, it holds up my 36c's to perfection. I hear Evan groan. He picks me up and throws me down on the bed. I bounce slightly and feel my breasts jiggle. His fingers unbutton the top of my jeans and then he lowers my zipper. His warm hands tickle my hips as he drags my jeans off and discards them on the floor. My matching knickers follow. I sit up and help him out of his own jeans and lick my lips when I see the erection straining against his boxers. He peels off his own tee and throws it behind him and then he pushes me back onto the bed.

I breathe a massive relaxed sigh and he hasn't even started yet. I'm booked in for the Heavenly Evan experience. Everything I've heard at the bar I'm now going to experience myself. I recall every sentence I've heard about the man to the forefront of my mind, starting with:

'Oh, that thing he does with his finger and his tongue…'

He pushes my knees up and opens my thighs wide. My core clenches as I see him hover over it. He closes his eyes and then opens them as he tongues me right *there*. My hips buck up off the bed. I love a man going down on me. Callum was never too keen. Evan feasts on me like I'm the most amazing lemon meringue pie. My clit, a stiff peak of meringue, and the lemon filling — well, I'm sure you get the picture. He swirls his tongue over my peak and then dips in to taste my filling. Then he adds a finger, while he laves my clit with his tongue. I don't know what the hell he touches with that finger as he swirls it around inside me, but I'd take a wild guess at my G-spot because I feel myself build in record time and then I explode all over his face.

I'm breathless, laid back against the pillow. "Fuck, Jesus, that. Oh my God, that."

The drawer is opened, and as I guessed, it houses his condom collection. A condom packet is torn by his teeth. He stands at the edge of the bed, shrugging off his boxers. You know how in books the woman always says, 'how the hell will I fit that in me?', well, HOW THE HELL WILL I FIT THAT IN ME?

'His cock is huge, isn't it?'

Yes, I answer, in reply to the past women at the bar. It is, I agree. He rolls the condom over his dick and then positions himself over me. For a moment, I tense. Oh my God, it's actually happening! Am I dreaming? Please, please, please, don't let this be a cruel dream that I'm going to wake from at any moment. Then he pushes against me. Hell, yeah, I'm not dreaming!

He inches in slowly, and I relax to accommodate him. I place my hands on his butt and feel it tighten with each slow thrust. His arse is taut. I resist giving it a little slap. Fully inside me, he then starts to pull out, almost sliding the whole way out before plunging back in again.

I feel a thrill all the way through my core. It travels into my breasts, up my back and into my brain. Everything is connected as I experience the best goddamn shag I've ever had, just as I knew I would.

'Did he do that thing with his finger in your butt hole?'

His hands are on my breasts, pinching and stroking. He kisses the side of my neck and I feel my skin goose bump. I make so many noises. All the groans and 'Oh fucks' that have escaped Evan's mouth have turned me on even more and I'm soaked down there. His thrusts quicken and my body rejoices in the feel of his movements. He places a finger at my clit and rubs there quickly. As my own orgasm hits I feel him tighten, and then groan as he spills out into the condom. He then relaxes, his body moving over to one side of me, so he's resting against me, half on and half off. He slips out of me, removing the condom, tying it and placing it on the floor. Then he pulls me against him.

'Did he do that thing with his finger in your butt hole?'

No. He didn't.

Why not?

Evan

She untangles herself from my arms and sits up.

"Evan, why didn't you stuck your finger in my butt hole as we were about to come?"

It's like a bucket of cold water has been thrown on me.

I sit up quickly, all of a sudden feeling quite sober and very awake.

"Pardon?"

She has her arms folded across her chest now, which blocks my view of her gorgeous tits.

"When all your previous women have spoken of your prowess, they always, *always*, go on and on about the finger in the butt hole. They said they came like freight trains when you did it. So why" – her jaw tenses – "have you not done that with me?"

You shagged Rachel.

You **shagged** Rachel.

YOU SHAGGED RACHEL.

YOU BROKE THE RULE.

Shit. Fuck. Wank. Bastard.

It's like a siren is going off in my head. WHOOP, WHOOP, WHOOP, WHOOP.

What is she going on about? Finger in her butt hole? Eh?

"Rachel. What are you talking about?"

"What you do with your moves. Your Heavenly Evan moves. I got the G-spot finger while you go down, the experience of your huge cock, but I didn't get the finger in butt hole. I was looking forward to it. All the women say they come so hard when you do that."

I shake my head as if I can get her words to fall out of my ears so I never heard them.

My moves?

Heavenly Evan?

Discussed? What, in public, or in private chats?

An awful realisation hits me. I shag them all the same. They all get one bout of me and I'm so used to my routine, I don't deviate from what gets me, and them, off. To the point where Rachel knew what she was getting before she got it and is now annoyed because I fucked her differently.

I put my head in my hands.

Oh my God.

"You're going to have to bonk me again, Evan, because there's no way I'm not knowing what that's like."

I move a hand away from one eye.

"Excuse me?"

She lies back on the bed. "You heard me, let's go."

I shake my head. "Rachel. I'm sorry, this has been a mistake. A drunken mistake. There's no way I would treat you like those other women. I should never have done this with you."

She screams. "Oh my God, why? Why am I so fucking different? Why can't I have your big cock in me? Why can't I have your finger in my ass? I don't want to be different, Evan. I want to be the same as the others."

"But you're not," I tell her, "and I made a promise I wouldn't do this with you."

"Why?" she asks, frustration evident in her tone.

"Because."

Rachel jumps out of bed. "Because, is not a fucking reason. I'm going to get washed and dressed."

She lands out of bed with a thump, which is a mighty feat for someone so slim, then storms off into the hallway, looking for the bathroom. "Where's the fucking bathroom, Evan?"

"It's downstairs," I tell her.

Thump.

Thump.

Thump.

For thirteen stairs.

Then, slam.

I hear the shower turn on. I lie back on the bed

realising just how much our screw has screwed us up.

Rachel

To say I'm fucked off is an understatement. I wash quickly, thankful that the practised act of Evan sex means there are guest towels laid out in the bathroom and some female shower gels and shampoos. I bet he even has fucking tampons in the cupboard.

I step out of the shower, wrap a towel around my head and another around my body and get ready to stomp back upstairs as I forgot to take my clothes with me. As I pass the front door something silver catches my eye and I grab it before going upstairs. Evan passes me as I reach his room. "I'm going to get cleaned up myself, then we'll talk."

"Talk. I don't recall any of your other lovers saying they talked. Except to try to give you their phone number on their way out of the door."

"Just give me a moment, Rach."

I wag a finger at him. "Do not *Rach* me. We are not friends right now."

He huffs and leaves the room.

I look around for somewhere to hide what I've stolen. Got it. There's a loose piece of carpet at the edge of the room and it fits under there nicely.

I get dressed, find a hairdryer, and dry my hair.

Evan returns. He's put on some lounge pants and an oversized tee. He sits on the edge of the bed.

"I'm so sorry, Rachel. I genuinely didn't know that women talked about me and that I had a set routine. I guess I'm just used to picking a woman up and doing my thing."

"Do you know what else they say?" Her lip curls.

I sigh. "Please, enlighten me."

"They say you seduce them, then you shag them, then you send them out on their arse."

I sigh again. "That's true. No repeats and my rule is no one stays."

"Why?"

"Because they're one-night stands. I don't do commitment. I don't want to encourage them."

"So, is that what I am? A one-night stand?"

"No, Rachel." I feel my heart clench as I get ready to say the words my brain screams at me not to say.

"You aren't a one-night stand. You shouldn't have happened. This was a mistake."

She punches the pillow. I thank Christ that it

isn't my face. I'd have been out for the count. Actually, I think I might feel better if she did lay me out. At least I'd escape the awful feeling in the pit of my stomach.

She's going to go home and tell her mother.

Then her mother is going to tell my mother.

Then I'm dead. I swore I wouldn't touch Rachel.

Something nags at the back of my mind. When I first saw Rachel when I was leaving the pub she said those words, but differently.

"Is that really what they say about me? Seduce. Shag. Send home?"

"Yes." She nods. "And I've no intention of joining them. I will not be part of the stand-drooling-at-Evan bar crowd."

I breathe a sigh of relief. "Oh, thank God. So, you get this was never supposed to happen? Can ours be seduce, shag, secret?"

"No, it fucking cannot."

I watch as she stands with a hand on her hip and repeats the words I heard earlier that night.

"I'm seduce." She holds up a finger.

"Shag." Finger number two.

"And stay the whole damn night. What are you going to do about that, hey? You broke your rules already. No finger in Rachel's ass, so get ready to break another. That no one stays the night. I'm going nowhere until I get the full Heavenly Evan experience."

"Well, that's not happening," I say and I rush at her, picking her up before she can realise what's happening and place her over my shoulder. Grabbing her bag as I turn to leave the room, I try to ignore the pert ass next to my head and I walk down the stairs towards the door.

Eh?

Where's my key?

WHERE'S MY FUCKING KEY?

"Where's my key, Rachel?" I demand.

"Somewhere you aren't finding it until I get my goddamn shag," she sasses.

I put her back on the floor.

"In fact, Mr Evan Hale." She leans against the door, hands once again folded over her chest. "I'm not leaving until a – I get my butt hole finger shag, and b – until you realise that" – she stabs my chest with her finger to enunciate every last word – "That. I. Am. The. One. For. You. Do you hear me? THE ONE. No more fucking about. So, get comfy, Mr Hale, because I intend for us to get intimately acquainted tonight. We have a lot of years to catch up on." She glares at me. God knows what I look like right now, my chin must be on the floor. "Okay, now that's clear, I think we'll start with a tour of this house. I need to get to know it better and I'm dying for a glass of water followed by a mug of steaming coffee. Come and show me where everything is in the kitchen, Evan."

I stand there for a moment, not moving. I need to know where that key is, so I'm going to have to play along until she either realises this is a mistake, or a glance from her eyes gives its location away. Looks like we're both on a mission this evening.

"What time do you not let them stay past?" she asks. "I'm sure the odd time you fell asleep afterward."

"Never. I've never slept and I won't tonight. You're not staying all night, Rachel."

"We'll see. You'd better make sure the coffee is strong if you don't intend to sleep all night. I'm staying until eight am. That will count as me having stayed the night and broken your rules. Then, if you're still being pig-headed, at least when I chat with all the girls in the pub and they talk about the ass finger, I'll be able to say I stayed the night and they'll all be jealous of me."

"Can you please stop going on about your ass? My finger is getting a complex."

"Hopefully though, you'll have come to your senses by then and realise that you need no other woman than me. That what you needed all along was right beside you, living next door, but you were just too blind to see it."

Oh, I was never too blind, Rach. Almost went blind with all my jacking off, but I saw you alright. Tonight is going to be the death of me.

My coffee needs to be very, very, strong because I can't risk falling asleep. I need that key. I need it as soon as I can, before she manages to do what she's set out to do and has me so I can't say no. I can't risk it not working out and me breaking her heart. I can't. I think too much of her. She could never be just a one-night stand, not mentally. But in real life, that's what I'm going to have to make her. I'll play her games and when she falls asleep — which she eventually will — I will leave. I'll find the key and a way out of my house. If only I knew where I'd put the damn window lock keys. One way or another, we are not staying the whole night together. Because if we do, it risks too damn much.

"I'd better show you the kitchen."

CHAPTER Four

COFFEE AND CONFESSIONS

Rachel

*H*mmm, this is going to be harder than I thought.

I look down at Evan's cock hanging free in his pants.

Rachel, you can't think of his cock every time you think of a word like hard.

Fuck, I just looked at it again.

So, in my dreams, it had always gone that we would do the dirty and he'd realise that I was the best bonk ever. We'd fall asleep in each other's arms, and I'd be there all night. The next morning, he would realise I was there, declare his undying love for me, and voila - happy ever after. Huge white wedding. Three children.

I was not expecting to be told I was a mistake and

to have the bloke doing his best to turf me out of his house. He's fooling no one if he thinks acting casual and lounging around is going to make me think he's accepted what I said. He's had a personality transplant, fake bastard. Oh no, I'm not fooled, not in the slightest. But, well, I may as well make the most of his easy-going manner, cos he's bound to become a right ratty twat when he wants to sleep and won't let himself.

I head into the kitchen. It's full of plain white units with a strip of black glossy bricks set between the worktop and upper cupboards. I spy the coffee machine in the corner and take out the bit that needs filling with water. I turn to Evan.

"Can you show me where you keep the pods, mugs, spoons, etc."

He smiles as if he couldn't think of anything nicer to do and opens every single cupboard to show me what's inside, including the inside of his fridge and freezer. As I expected, Evan lives on microwave meals, jars of curry, and pasta, and two-minute microwave rice. He gets his nutrition from his Sunday lunch at his mother's. How the hell he's maintained such a great body must be a testament to the large fruit bowl on the kitchen table, overflowing with oranges and apples. I take out two mugs from a cupboard which I wash in the sink because I don't trust a twenty-five-year-old bachelor boy to clean properly.

Then we both spot it, at the same time. There's a key in the back door. Not a chance mate. I leap for the door at the same time as Evan. The key is in my hand and Evan forces my wrist around until he prises it out of my grip. So, I poke him in the eye.

"Holy fucking Jesus Christ, you crazy bitch. I'm blind."

He's not blind, but he is keyless. He dropped it clutching for his eye, and I put it down my knickers. The only way he's getting it is by getting in my pants. Either way, I win.

He takes his hand away, his eye red and watering. He shakes his head in disbelief. "Why would you do such a thing?"

"You're trying to get me out of the house. I'm not going anywhere."

"You can't get home from my garden. It's fenced off."

"Then why did you jump for the key? I firmly believe you'd have locked me outside until I agreed to go home."

"I was going to put it out of your crazy ass way so that in the event of a fire, we could get out without being burned alive. Just in case you've swallowed the front door one, and I've got to wait for nature to take its course before I get it back."

"Ew, I have so not done that, you sicko. But don't worry, to get to the kitchen one, the fire needs to be in my pants."

He looks at my jeans, eyes wide. "You put my kitchen door key down your knickers?"

"Yup. Want to open the door, you're going to have to open my legs."

"You're disgusting."

"I aim to please."

"You can keep the kitchen door key. I don't need it. I will have a coffee though. I'm starting to get a headache, I can't think why."

Five minutes later we have two fresh coffees, and Evan takes me around the rest of the house. "So, this is the living room. As you can see I've no dining room. The kitchen does both. Other than that, downstairs, there's the bathroom which you've already seen, and a small utility room which, to be honest, is full of bikes and the crap my mum gave me when I moved in."

The living room is a decent size and quite square in shape. His leather couch looks like it could do with a good clean. It has cup marks on the seats.

Blokes can be disgusting. "Have you got some wipes so I can clean the sofa?" I ask.

He looks at me like I've mentioned that I'm married to an alien.

I roll my eyes and push past him, back into the kitchen where I grab his tea towel and wet half of it under the hot tap. I then come back and clean the sofa.

"I'm surprised your mum lets you get away with keeping a pigsty of a house."

"My mum doesn't come here. That's why I go there on a Sunday. Keeps her sweet and away from here, plus I get a decent meal for free every week."

"I was surprised when you moved," I tell him. "One moment you were there, the next you were gone. I thought with you going to Uni in Sheffield you'd have stayed at home and made the most of the free rent."

Stay at home. Yeah. That had been the plan...

CHAPTER Five

LOSING THINGS

Evan

I managed, though it was a struggle, to live next door to the ever-emerging beauty of Rachel Summers. The main saving grace was that she loved gardening and was forever dressed in a grubby pair of cargo pants and a baggy tee-shirt, with her hair in a ponytail and her face and hands covered in dirt. Still looked sexy as fuck but it was toned down.

Everything went wrong when she turned seventeen, and her mother decided she could now drink and visit nightclubs. A fact I only found out when a drunken Rachel came up to me in such a club, inebriated, in a night not dissimilar to the one we'd just had.

September 2010

"Evan. Evan. Thank god you're here."

*I swing around to find myself face to face with a woman who looks like Rachel from next door. I take in the short black dress, the fuck-me heels, the smoky eyes, poker-red lips, and my dick salutes. Then I realise it **is** Rachel. Rachel Summers is in front of me, in front of every sex-mad man here, in this club, looking entirely fuckable. She's pissed as a fart and can hardly stand up straight, and she looks panicked. Hell, has someone attacked her?*

"Rachel. Is everything okay?"

"I've lost my phone. Evan, can you help me find it? My mum will kill me. She only let me come out with the promise I would keep my phone on me and let her know as soon as I phoned a taxi home, so she knew when to expect me. She's shitting herself that I've come out drinking and now I can't reassure her because I've lost my damn phone," she says, shaking the exact phone she's talking about in front of me.

"Er, Rachel. Is this your phone?" I ask her.

She stares at it, a look of complete amazement crossing her face.

"Yes. Yes, it is. Oh, thank you, Evan. Where was it? Oh, I'm so happy you found it."

I'm almost knocked over as Rachel throws her arms around me. "Oh, thank you, Evan, you've saved my life."

I'm instantly aware that her boobs are squished against my chest. She looks up at me with her large brown doe eyes, and I'm about three seconds from sticking my dick down her throat so they can look at me like that while she makes me come in her mouth.

One, two. I push her away as if she's on fire.

She stumbles backwards and almost falls over.

Damn it.

"Rachel. Who did you arrive with?"

"Keeley. But she's in the corner with Aiden, her boyfriend. I'm a goose bump."

"You mean a gooseberry?"

"That's what I said. Are you all right, Evan? You look a bit clammy and flushed." She leans over and feels my forehead. "Do you feel all right?" She slides her hand down the side of my face. "Lovely Evan, finding my phone."

"Okay, let's get that taxi called," I tell her. I need the safety of a cab so that my own actions are being watched and I can get her home safely.

I get her to give me her phone so I can text her mother and then I take her home.

Her mother opens the door and shakes her head as Rachel wobbles up the path. "Thanks, Evan, for bringing her home. I warned her not to get in this state. She could have ended up in real trouble. Thank goodness we have a well-behaved gentleman living next door. I'd better get her inside and get some water down her."

Adam appears, rubbing sleep out of his eyes. "Oh dear. Well, I guess we all do it at least once, hey? I'll help you get her up to her room, Sally."

With that, the door closed and I went back to my own house.

The next time I went clubbing I lost my virginity to a woman with long dark hair in an alley at the back of the club.

While, no doubt, Rachel's room spun around, it was my thoughts that did. Thoughts of her pert breasts against my chest. Her arms around my neck. Her hand caressing my face. I realised that night that I couldn't carry on living next door to Rachel anymore. It was too much. Men were going to come on to her and date her, and I didn't want to witness any of it. So, I moved into digs with some Uni mates. I only had to see Rachel a fraction of the time then, when our paths crossed in bars or clubs.

My pattern of serial one-night stands started after that night. I'm not sure how many times I imagined they were Rachel. Then she started working at the Nag's Head, and I had to get used to seeing her regularly again. Seeing her dating other men. So, I carried on with my one-night stands and hoped that one day sooner, rather than later, I'd click with one of them, make a connection that broke the torch I carried for Rachel Summers. But it never did.

"Earth calling Evan. Where'd you go then? Not getting tired, are you?"

"Definitely not," I say, sitting up on the couch. "I'm wide awake," I state emphatically, taking a large swig of my coffee. "To answer your question," I add, "I moved out of my parents' house because I had manly needs to meet and I couldn't do that in my parents' home."

"Ah, you needed a shag pad."

"Something like that."

"I missed you when you left," she says. "It was weird not seeing you around, emptying the bins, or having to put up with the crap music that used to boom from your bedroom window."

"I did not play crap music."

"That is entirely debatable. But we'll discuss musical likes and dislikes when we have our getting to know each other better session."

"Our what?"

"In order to stay the night, we can either go to sleep, or I have a dazzling array of entertainment planned," she says, "including watching a film, a getting to know you session, and a sex Q&A. Lots of things to ensure we stay awake all night long, or..." She tilts her head at me. "We can go to bed and go to sleep."

"At some point, I'll find that key," I tell her. "And you will be on your way in a taxi."

"Well, until then, what DVD shall we watch?"

"There's a cupboard full of them." I point towards it. "Open those doors and knock yourself out."

She turns to me with a beaming smile.

I leap up. "No, actually, this is my place. We'll watch a film of my choosing." Christ, I have a few chick flicks for when I have to work a bit harder at getting in a girl's knickers, like The Notebook. The last thing I want is Rachel crying on my shoulder. I need her at the other end of the sofa.

"Whatever," she says dismissively. "If it makes you feel more in control of the situation, which you most certainly are not, go right ahead and choose."

I keep quiet and let her think she's won, because I'm mightily relieved that I distracted her from when she said she missed me.

CHAPTER Six

TERMINATED

Evan

Women are the devil.

I celebrate my choice of DVD with another strong coffee. I'm going to do nothing but want to piss soon. I chose *Terminator 2*. The one where Arnie is the good guy and has to fight that bloke whose arm can turn into dangerous weapons. Enough action to keep me awake with the adrenaline of the plot. Moving right to the other edge of the sofa, well away from where Rachel is sitting, I rest my arm on the chair arm and settle down to watch it.

Throughout the film, I can see her keep turning to me. From the corner of my eye, I see the frustration on her face that I've not fallen asleep so she can win this battle of her staying the night. It's become a simple competition to me now. I can't even remember the main reasons behind it anymore. I shouldn't really give a shit if she does stay the night, I've still buggered things up, but hey I'm male, competitive, and she is not winning this. No way.

All is well until the metal man melts and Rachel starts to cry. She fucking starts crying? What the hell?

The bad guy is being destroyed. This is where you punch the air and celebrate as he becomes drops of metal. Hell, I know that in a few minutes he'll manage to drag himself back together before the definite ending of the film.

Rachel shuffles along the sofa towards me and throws her face onto my arm, wetting my arm with her tears. She raises her head and sniffles. "This is so sad. He can't help it. He's a robot that's been programmed to kill them. Why can't they just reprogramme him? Why do they have to melt him down?" Then once again, she throws herself onto my arm with noisy sobs.

"Er, there, there. It's only a movie, Rachel." I pat her head, not knowing what else to do. I've never seen such an emotional reaction to an action flick and wonder if she's due her period, as that's when my mother would go a bit crazy.

After a couple of minutes, she lifts her head but

remains snuggled into my side. She presses closer to me and fastens her hands around my arm.

"Sorry about that. Thank you. I don't know what it is about that film. It gets me every time." She looks at me, and I realise that she's snuggled up with her blowjob gaze fixed on me. Shit, how do I get her back to the other edge of the sofa?

Perfectly, that's when a fart decides to make an appearance. Sometimes coffee has that effect on me. I let a silent, but hopefully deadly one out.

Rachel lifts herself a bit, and I can see she's trying not to breathe in. Ha, take that and move right over there.

"Oh, Evan. I'm sorry I've wet your shirt. If you take it off, I'll go and hairdryer it for you."

What? Damn this woman.

My arm is rather disgustingly wet from her watering eyes, and God forbid her nose ran.

"I'll get another one," I tell her. I need to move away from this smell I've created, it's lingering.

"I'll do it. I saw where you kept them."

She leaves the room and goes upstairs. What is she up to? I doubt this is just to escape a potent fart smell.

She returns with a new lounge top for me and leans over. "Let's take this one off then." As she moves closer, I see quite clearly that while she was upstairs she has removed her bra, so as she leans towards me to take off my shirt I get a direct view of her tits.

I leap back on the sofa. "Get to the other side, now. I get what you're doing. You're trying to seduce me again. Not a chance. Even if you have got a great rack."

She backs off pouting.

"Give it up, Rachel. Give me the key. Let's get you a taxi and we can all go to bed and go to sleep - separately."

She tilts her chin upward. "I don't think so, Evan. I think I'll stay right here. You go up though if you want. If you're tired."

"Me. Nah, I'm absolutely fine." I try to stifle a yawn but the more I think about it, the more it makes my face stretch and hurt with the force of it.

"Great. We'll have a good catch up chat then, because really, what sort of a woman am I that sleeps with a man she doesn't know that much about anymore? It'll appease my conscience if you answer a few questions."

I sit back. This is going to be a long-arsed night. Maybe I can bore her with my answers?

"Fire away."

"Why did you never come around when we had

barbecues and stuff? I was always stuck there with my family and yours, unless Mum let me have a mate round. I felt stupid."

I shrug. "It wasn't my thing to hang around with the folks, the neighbours, and the little kid from next door, so I stayed home instead."

Translation: You started wearing vest tops and cut off shorts, and I wouldn't have needed a kebab stick at the barbecue cos the meat could have hung straight from my cock.

"What made you train as an architect?"

"Seriously? You want to know why I do the job I do?"

"Yes, it's part of who you are."

"It really isn't," I tell her. "A teacher suggested it. I couldn't be arsed to look around, so I applied. Job done.

Translation: I had a stupid teenage idea that I'd build you a house with lots of garden outbuildings so you could run your own business.

"When did you lose your virginity?"

"I was eighteen." *And it was all your fault.*

"How many lovers have you had?"

"Hey, this Q&A," I interrupt. "Is there only you that can ask the questions? Perhaps I want to know stuff about you?"

"Like what?"

"Like, what time are you going home."

She sighs. "I've told you. I'm going nowhere. Now, how many lovers have you had?"

I have a think. *One a week since I was eighteen and now I'm twenty-five. So roughly 7 x 52. Jesus! That many!*

"Bout, erm... fifty?"

"Fifty?" she says. "I've only slept with three people."

Thank goodness I lied, but as her words hit home, I feel my fist clench.

"Three people? I thought you'd only been with Callum."

"No. First, I got drunk and had a bit of an experiment with one of my college mates. I'm counting it as we did a bit of kissing and foreplay and she did stay the night at mine. We laughed about it the next day, realised we needed dicks in our lives."

I've gone still as a statue. Dear God, please, please, please, take this visual from my mind. Rachel getting it on with another woman. Jeez, I can see it now in full porno style glory. I'm going to have to go to the bathroom in a minute and rub one out. *Imagine shagging Arnie instead, quick, think of Arnie with his battered Terminator head. Come on, son, down you go, down you go.*

"Anyway, then I properly lost my virginity to Tony, my driving instructor. We did it in a country lane in the back of the car. I felt so dirty."

If I knew where to find this instructor, I would punch his lights out for taking advantage of a young woman.

"Of course, it comes out in my sexual fantasies now, where it's not with Tony, and it's hot." She winks.

Terminator head. Terminator head.

"Then, of course, I slept with Cal, but you know that already."

"Yes. Well, thank you for letting me know. Next question, more coffee? I think we need more coffee." I run out of the room.

Rachel

I'm dying to laugh. Well, my fake crying fit didn't work so I thought I'd make up a lesbian lover and a sex in the country fantasy instead. He doesn't need to know that I've only slept with Callum. Not at the side of all the women he's slept with and fifty, I think, is a very conservative estimate on his part. There's no wonder he knows exactly what to do in bed. He's had so much bloody practice. I feel inadequate at the side of him. Maybe I should have had lots of lovers so I would know how to put a condom on with my mouth etc. I should have tried sticking my finger up *his* bum. I've heard men like that. I'm just so bloody, well, virginal-like. Don't get me wrong, Callum and I did it in different positions, we went down on each other. It's just wasn't very scintillating. I had thought it was alright until tonight. Now I realise what more I could expect from being the lover of Evan Hale. I want an apprenticeship as his sex slave. That tent in his shorts before he escaped to the kitchen was hilarious. I'll have to think up some more sexy scenarios for when he returns.

His pathetic attempts to get me away from him are amusing. Does he think Callum never farted? We all trump; that's not going to shift me. Wait til he cops a load of me after garlic bread.

I turn the TV over from the DVD channel back to the usual Freeview. There's nothing much on at this time in the morning, but then I see the fitness channel. Come on, you must have seen those sometimes. They sell fitness machines that look like bad sex toys. This is perfect. I sit back and wait for Evan to return from the kitchen. I'm a lot more relaxed now as well, without my bra. I hid the kitchen key inside it upstairs, so I no longer have an uncomfortable key in my knickers. I relax against the sofa, ready to play.

Evan

Rachel has put on some stupid sales channel. A man and a woman have a piece of plastic between their thighs which they are opening and shutting. Yep, basically, it's like fitness porn. The woman is fit, in more ways than one, and she's clenching her thighs for all she's worth, while the cameraman zooms in on her pelvis. I mean, I wouldn't even want payment for that job.

"Can you switch this over, Rachel? It's a little boring, to be honest."

Rachel puts her legs on the couch and starts clenching them together, then letting them fall apart and clenching again. "Hmmm, I might buy one. I can see how it can tighten your core."

Help me God, this is almost impossible. I really need you right now.

"Sit up and turn the channel over." My words come out a little harsh.

"Okay." She rolls her eyes at me, then settles on a channel selling clothes. I've read about these in the papers lately. Some of them have been noted to look a bit peaky in the nipple department.

"You can see her tits through that top, can't you?" exclaims Rachel.

I look and gulp. "Erm, yes. She must be cold."

"I'm not, I'm flipping roasting," Rachel says. "It must be all that hot coffee, or you've got the heating on." She stands up, peels off her jeans and lays on my sofa in just her panties and tee-shirt. The tee-shirt that I now notice has pointy nipples poking through it, just like the woman on TV.

Rachel looks at me, a glint in her eye, and then she swings her legs back up on the sofa and does the thigh clench thing again. "Do you think I've got the movement right, only I could do with working on my thighs."

I can't even answer. My mouth is so dry.

It's no good. My blood has drained from my brain and into my once again tented todger.

Rachel 11,000. Evan 0.

CHAPTER
Seven

DRASTIC MEASURES

Evan

*I*t's just gone five-thirty am. I'm horny as fuck, and I am seriously done with all this shit. I've tried to get her to go home and see that I'm not the one for her but she isn't taking a blind bit of notice. It's going to have to be the love-em-and-leave-em approach after all. I have to hope and pray that she does not tell her mother any of this. So, therefore, I need to do things that she *can't* tell her mother.

"Right, that's it. You win."

She narrows her eyes. "What are you up to now? You're not going to just give in."

"I seriously fucking am giving in. I quit trying to stay awake."

She looks at me, a satisfied smirk on her face.

"You're letting me stay the night?"

"Yes! That's what I just said. I need my fucking sleep, and you are seriously giving me goddamn blue balls. So, get that fit arse back into my bedroom because I'm going to tap it."

"Hurrah!" she shouts and runs upstairs.

How is she still so awake? I'm dead on my feet. I'm going to give her the shag of the century and then somehow, I've got to stay awake while getting *her* to fall asleep. All of my moves need to be in play. *All* of them.

"Right. You're getting the Heavenly Evan special, and I'm going to talk you through it. You haven't overheard all my secrets," I tell her.

She stands in the bedroom, peels off her underwear and sits propped up on the pillows. She lets her legs drop apart.

Fucking hell.

"Come get me." She pats the side of the bed.

The massage

"Sometimes women aren't that relaxed when they get in my bed. They need a little help to get in the mood, so I often start with a massage. Turn over."

Rachel flips over so she's laid on her stomach and I sit astride her back. I lean over into my bedside drawer and get some massage oil. I warm it in my palms and then beginning at Rachel's neck, I begin to massage it in. I feel her shoulders loosen as I work my thumbs over her flesh. Maybe she'll fall asleep now and save me the rest of it, although I realise that now I have the chance to shag Rachel once more, I don't want her to fall asleep. Not just yet. "Now, as you may notice, the massage is enjoyable, but have you also noticed that my stiff dick is resting on your back?"

"Hell, yeah," answers Rachel.

"Well, that's my first move in letting them know what's coming next. You see, I've given them a lovely massage. Turn over."

Rachel turns over, so I'm facing her fucking amazing tits. I add some more massage oil and run my hands down her neck and then stroke and tease her breasts with my oily hands. "Now, the woman's focus has to be on my dick, right?"

"Totally," Rachel says, running her tongue around her lips. "You can't miss it. It's right there." She fastens her hand around my cock.

"You've got it. So now I usually get a little hand action and sometimes..."

Rachel shuffles down and fastens her mouth around my cock. I buck slightly into her throat.

"You got it, baby. Sometimes they suck me off."

I let her mouth envelope me in warmth for a few minutes, and then I pull out. "Time to move on."

That thing with my tongue and finger.

"Want to have a woman think you're the best lover, ever? Find their G-spot. I'm well practised in locating the holy grail. Also, I should win awards for my oral techniques as all my practice has made me perfect."

"Bigheaded, much?"

I push my tongue into her pussy.

"Oooohhh."

I lift my head up. "You were saying?"

She pushes my head back down. "As you were, I need more to be able to assess your performance."

I run my tongue up and down her wet heat, then I suck her clit into my mouth, giving it the odd little bite. She moans and raises her hips off the bed. I push my tongue inside her opening and back out, in and back out. I notice she grasps the bedcovers tightly in her hands.

I raise my head back up. "Now, you've already experienced my tongue and finger trick once tonight, so I'm going to give you the extra-minty version."

"What?" Rachel says, confused. Her eyes are dazed with lust. "Don't leave me like this. I need to come so bad."

"And you will." I move to my bedside drawer and take out a mint, which I put in my mouth.

"You don't have time for a snack, Evan. Get back down there."

I wink at her. "Give me a minute and all will be forgiven."

I chomp the mint and make my way back down between her legs. Then I tongue her clit and suck on it before licking all up her heat. The mint will cause a cool and spicy sensation to hit her sweet spots.

"Oh my good God, Evan. Don't stop," she squeals.

Her hands go back to gripping the bedsheets, and this time, I put two fingers together and sink them into her depths, curling to hit that G. Her core shudders around me as her body takes her over the edge. Her whole body is shaking from her orgasm, and she runs a hand through her hair. "Oh, my."

I flick her clit again, knowing how sensitive it will be.

She moves up the bed out of my reach. "Don't touch it again yet. It's too much. I need to come down."

"Nope." I shake my head at her. "While your body is still coming down, it's time for this."

Introducing my massive member (again)

So, they talk about how large I am down the pub? Good to know. Thought I was ample in that department but can't say I do a compare and contrast with my mates. Some of them could be growers. Mine's kind of okay from the off, although right now, it's a deep purple and threatening to make me pass out as all my blood seems to be concentrated in that area. I can literally hear it in my ears screaming, 'Let me in. Let me in. Let me in.'

"I'm clean. Are you on the pill? Only I want to go bare."

"Do you go bare with other women?"

"No." I shake my head. "You're about to get an experience no woman has had before, so you can share *that* in the pub."

"Cool. Yes, I'm on the pill."

I realise then that the reason she's on the pill is because that twat bastard Callum has shagged her. It's rather unfair to be pissed off that Rachel's had other lovers given my own history, but I can't help it. I wanted to be first. I have to ask her..."

"Have you done this before? Been ridden bare."

"No, I haven't. Now can you get on with the shag pl—"

I sink into her before she finishes her sentence."

-ease. Oh, my."

I rotate my hips a little as I plunge in and out of her. The feeling of being bare, of feeling the warmth from her sweet pussy, is immeasurable. For a split second, I imagine Rachel being in my bed every day, before the realisation hits that she can't be mine.

The finger in the butt hole (that caused all the grief in the first place).

I don't want to do it. I don't want Rachel getting a repeat performance of everything I ever did with another woman. I want lots of firsts with her. This is going to kill me. But I run my digit in her wetness, and as I bring us to the brink with my thrusts I meet her final demand, and the finger goes where she wanted it. What does she do? Pulls my hand away.

"I've changed my mind about that. I don't want to be just another notch on a bedpost. Lie back on the bed, Evan."

I move her over, and she sits astride me. Then she raises herself up. A hand runs through her hair and then she trails a finger down her face, running it through the edge of her lip and biting it. She sucks on her finger, and as she begins to rotate up, down and around on my dick, she gets that wet finger, and she plays with herself. I thrust into her like a woodpecker trying to fell a tree. She moves her other hand to play with one of her tits. Jesus Christ. I grab the back of her arse as my balls tighten and I come inside her. I buck, my final orgasmic spasms taking place while still inside her warmth.

"Oh my God, Rachel. Oh my God."

"I know. It's so good, isn't it? We're so good together. I knew we would be. I'm better than them, aren't I? You did your routine with me. Was I better than them all?"

I feel the need to be honest. She just let me cum in her. "There's no comparison."

"And we did new things too. Plus" – she looks at the clock – "It's six-thirty am, and I'm tired. Are you tired? Are you going to finally let me stay the night?"

"I am," I tell her, and I wrap myself around her, letting her snuggle into my chest I trail my hands down her body: down her arms, her neck, her hips, and she does it. She falls asleep, and I have to keep pinching myself to keep awake, but I need to know she has fallen asleep. After about twenty minutes, I move my arm to test the situation. She's dead to the world.

I slide out of bed, grab my clothes and sneak downstairs. I'm now going to prove I'm the biggest bastard ever so that Rachel can move on. My mother will be awake as she gets up for work at this time, so I'm going to head over to hers. Rachel will wake up and realise that we did not stay the whole night together.

She did not break my rule.

I just hope I don't break her heart.

Rachel

I hear a noise. Opening my eyes, for a moment I wonder where I am. Then I remember. I'm at Evan's. In his bed after a glorious bout of sex. I realise Evan isn't wrapped around me anymore. He probably got too hot. I turn over to look at him.

He's not there.

I look at the clock. Eight minutes to seven.

He's left.

I know if I look at the side of my bed, I'll find my discarded bra unwrapped and the key gone. There obviously is a way out from the back garden. He just didn't want me to know.

I lie back.

We didn't stay the whole night together.

He doesn't care.

We have nothing.

A pain hits my chest. I've become another of Evan's floosies. I was fooling myself. I didn't want what the others had had. I wanted what they'd had and more. Then I stupidly let him know that, and he's run away scared. Evan must not be capable of a relationship. Why I didn't realise that when he paraded one-night stand after one-night stand in front of me, I don't know.

I'm an idiot.

That's it for me. A tear escapes my eye.

I'm done with Sheffield. I need to move on. I can't go back to my bar job. There's no way I can watch a further parade of women. My heart hurts. I need to move away from my mother's. It's time I did anyway, and now my relationship with Callum is finished, I'd be under her's and Adam's feet. It's not fair. They need time alone. A new place to live, a new town or city, a new career, and eventually, way, way down the line, a new man. A mix of Evan and Callum. A man who can rock my world in bed, but wants to give me the moon. That's what I deserve. I'm not the first woman to have her heart broken by a dickhead. Look at my Mum. My father was a charmer until he smacked her. At least I've only been embarrassed, not the victim of domestic violence. See? It's not so bad, I tell myself. I move out of bed. A massive yawn stretches my lips wide. I've had just over twenty minutes sleep all bloody night. Yet, I'm wide awake. I put my bra and panties back on, then head downstairs to use the bathroom and dress in the rest of my clothes. Finally, I walk back upstairs to get the front door key from under the carpet. With a final look at the rumpled bed and with a sigh, I bound down the stairs, open the door and move outside. I post the key through the letterbox.

Then I make my way to the bus stop and head on home. I feel like karma is getting her own back on me for dumping Callum, but it wouldn't have been fair to lead him on.

Yes, I think a fresh start is exactly what I need.

CHAPTER
Eight

HUMAN ERROR

Evan

I really don't think I should have driven. I'm possibly still over the legal limit of alcohol, and I'm ready to fall asleep at any second. I need to get in my old house and crash in my old bedroom. It's now a spare room. I don't give two fucks that it's now done up in vintage pink and blue bedlinen. A bed is a bed and right now the back of the car would do.

I knock at the back door, making my mum jump a foot. She comes over and opens it.

"Jesus, Evan. I'd quite like to make my fiftieth birthday. You gave me a bloody heart attack."

"Can I crash in my old room, Mum?"

Her mouth curves up at the corner. "What's up with your own house?"

"I've got a girl there, Mum, and she won't leave. She even stole my key."

My mum blows out her cheeks, then releases. "And you've left her in your house on her own. She could steal everything. Are you mad?"

"Nah, she won't. I know her. She'll be pissed off and put the key through the letterbox when she goes home. At least I don't have a pet bunny." I laugh. Then I sit at the table and think about it. Will she though? Or will she be that pissed off she takes the scissors to my clothes or sews fish into my curtains?" This *is* Rachel we're talking about.

"You've gone very pale, Evan." Mum sits down beside me and plonks a mug of coffee on the table. "Right. Out with it and no bullshit. You've got one minute to come clean. Remember, no secrets. So, whatever dick move you've made, I need to know right now. Then never mind sleeping here, you need to get back to your house and make sure you've not been robbed or had your house set on fire."

I sigh. "I slept with Rachel."

My mum looks me straight in the eye. "Next door Rachel?"

"Yep."

Mum looks confused but not shocked. "So why

would you want her to leave, and why have you left her in the house by herself?"

"Because, Mum. I messed up. You told me to leave Rachel alone, remember? And I did. I really did. I left her alone for years and years, but last night I had too much alcohol, and she didn't get engaged to Callum, and-"

"She turned Callum down?" My mum punches a fist in the sky. "Whoop! Oh, Sally will have a party. She can't stand him."

"Are you listening to me, Mum? I slept with Rachel."

"Well, I'm surprised it hasn't happened before now, love, to be honest, the way you're always mooning about over one another. Me and Sally thought you'd have got together by now. We wondered why you hadn't."

"Because you told me not to," I shout.

"Keep your voice down, your dad's still in bed," she says. Just as she used to do when I was a teenager getting ready for school. "What on earth are you talking about? You're a grown man. I can't tell you who to date."

"Mum. You said it when I was fifteen. To leave Rachel alone."

"Oh my God, Evan," she replies. "Of course, I

did. She was fourteen, you were fifteen. I used to be a fourteen-year-old girl. I didn't want you falling out with her and ruining the camaraderie between us and next door over a hormonal urge on your part. But you're an adult now, that's different. It's up to you who you date. You and Rachel are grown-ups."

I sit back in my chair and drink the whole mug of coffee.

"Oh my God. I left Rachel in my bed. I left her thinking she isn't good enough for me. That's she's just another one-night stand."

My mum folds her arms across her chest. Oh shit. "Repeat that again, Evan, so we can be clear. You've been having one-night stands? I thought I taught you to be respectful?"

I find I don't need the coffee to keep me awake as my mother gets up to the sink, fills her mug up with cold water and throws it straight in my face.

"What the hell, Mum?" I jump back.

"I promised to never lay a hand on you, and right now I want to strangle you, so instead I've thrown water. I can't believe what you've done. Get back to that bloody house of yours before she wakes up." She comes over to me and shoves me. "Right now, Evan."

I dash to the door, ready to race home, but my mum's not finished.

"You sort this out. It's your life. I guess I've no right really to judge how you conduct it. But Rachel's a lovely girl and deserves better than she's getting."

"I know that, Mum. I've bloody well cocked up big style. But you told me to leave her alone."

"Are you blaming me for the situation? Did I sleep with Rachel and run away?" She points at the door. I don't need telling again. I'm on my way.

Rachel

I wander up the road towards my house. I hope my mum and Adam are still in bed because I don't want them to witness my walk of shame and I don't want my mum to see my face. I will never tell her what happened between Evan and me. I'm too embarrassed, and I don't want to cause any trouble between my mum and Hazel. No, it's best if I keep quiet about the whole thing. Hopefully, I'll be moving on soon. I only have to serve a week's notice at the pub, which I'll do because Dan is amazing and I want a good reference from him. I might even consider running my own pub. Something I never thought about before. Suddenly, the world doesn't seem as bleak, but full of opportunity. Like diving in a bucket of grapes (which I loathe) and coming out with a bottle of wine. Right now, my grapes are sour.

So, I'm at the bottom of my path when the very man I wish to avoid dashes out of his mother's house. I ignore him and carry on walking.

"Rachel," he shouts. "Wait. I can explain."

I turn around. From this angle, I can see his car parked behind a large white van. Very nicely obscured while I walked down the road, giving me no advanced warning that the shithead was here.

I won't show him any emotion. I turn around and put my key in the lock. I go into my own home, closing it softly behind me.

Evan

Oh, this is bad. Very fucking bad.

The Rachel I know gets very angry when hard done by, when annoyed.

I just received a blank look.

Totally blank. Empty. Devoid of all emotion.

Either she doesn't care about me, or I've completely broken her. Emotional numbness.

I can't stand it. I want to rewind time. Go back to tonight. In fact, back to the nightclub. Back to before all the one-night stands. I would take Rachel home that drunken night when she was seventeen, and I would see how she was the next day and ask her on a date. She'd never have been touched by another man, and I'd have been only ever hers.

This won't do. She can be my first at other things.

I hurtle up her path and bang on her front door. I don't care that it's early on a Saturday morning. I need to talk to Rachel, and I need to talk to her now.

After a few minutes, Sally opens the door looking bleary-eyed and wrapped in her robe.

Her eyes widen when she looks at me. "Evan. Is everything okay?"

"Can I speak to Rachel, please?"

She puts a hand on her chest. "Jesus, Evan, you scared the life out of me. I thought something had happened with your mum. You're all, like, panicked looking. Are you sure you're all right? What do you want Rachel for?"

Rachel stands in the doorway behind her mother. "Don't let him in. He's not welcome here anymore." She's tied her hair back in a ponytail, and she has a smear of dirt on her forehead. She's obviously been taking her anger out on the garden. That's better. She needs to be pissed off at me. I see that she's not blank after all.

"What's going on, Rachel?" asks Sally.

"We've fallen out," says Rachel. "I put up with him and stayed civil all the time he lived next door, but I'm fed up of living a lie. I think Evan Hale is a complete fucking turd. He treats women like shit, probably cos he's so familiar with it being A HUGE STEAMING DOLLOP OF MANURE." With that, she turns on her heel and heads back out into the garden.

Sally stands in the doorway, her mouth dropped open.

"Sally. Please let me in. Give me five minutes, and if she still wants me to leave, I'll go."

"I don't know, Evan, she seems pretty mad. Might be better to come back another day."

"I have things to say, Sally, and she needs to hear them now."

Sally sighs. "Five minutes, Evan. Then I'm afraid I'll have to ask you to leave."

"Thanks, Sally." I kiss her cheek as I dash past her and out into their back garden.

All these years and I've only ever seen this garden through my bedroom window.

I walk down the path towards the vegetable

patch at the very bottom of the garden where Rachel is digging vegetables up with gusto.

She stops and waves the spade at me. "Do not come any nearer."

"Rachel. Please, we need to talk. I made a mistake."

"Damn right you did. Had a top woman in your bed and you chose to walk away from her. You're a fucking idiot, now *leave*."

I take a step closer to her.

She frees a huge mound of potatoes, and leaves, stalks, roots, and potato come flying at my head. The whole lot lands atop my head and dirt runs down and off my face.

I'm a real life fucking Mr Potato Head.

"Come on, Evan. It's best you leave." Sally's voice comes from behind me. "I know from experience that there's no reasoning with Rachel when she's in a temper."

I turn to her. "When she calms down, will you tell her I'm sorry, and that I'm not giving up."

She nods, and I walk back through the house where Adam escorts me out of the front door. I drive home, and despite having not slept all night, I can't sleep and pace the house thinking of my night with Rachel.

CHAPTER Nine

I WANT WHAT SHE'S HAVING

Rachel

I sleep away the rest of the day until I have to get ready for my shift. Saturday night. I'm glad. It's the busiest night of the week, and I won't have time to worry about Evan Hale and the fact that I now need to leave Sheffield. Maybe I won't. Perhaps he should leave. Let's face it, he must have shagged half the population of Waterthorpe by now so he should move on to fresh pastures to swing his dick.

I look at my jeans and tee and think sod it. Instead, I put on a tight black lacy dress, tons of makeup and half pin up my hair. I tong the rest so curls fall around my face. If he dares to show his face in the Nag's Head tonight, he can jolly well see what he's missing. What he chose to turn down. My mind wanders to Callum. I know how shit he must feel now, and even worse, we'd been dating for a year. He imagined spending his life with me, and I turned him down. He was a good bloke, just not someone who set my heart on fire. I made the right choice though. I'm not settling. It wouldn't be fair to him. Maybe out there is a woman who will feel for him like I feel for Evan.

Correction.

Felt for Evan.

Past tense. You've got to move on, lass.

I feel very self-conscious as I walk into the bar and half the male heads turn to stare at me.

"Whoo, Rachel's sister, where's Rachel?" yells Dan.

"Very funny," I reply.

"Well you look hot, is that for lover boy's attention?"

"No, it most certainly is not," I spit out.

He holds his hands up. "Okay, okay. Thought you two had finally got together. He's done a Heavenly Evan on you, has he?"

"How do you know…?"

"I hear the same things you do, Rachel. However,

I also see him staring at you when you're not looking. It's been going on for years now. I also see you looking at him. I thought when I saw you last night that you'd finally stopped pissing about. So, what happened?"

"It was a mistake. It won't be happening again. There will be no more staring at Evan Hale from me. I'm dressed up because I'm moving on."

"Right, you'll not be interested to know that he's just come in then."

I stand up straighter and stick my chest out and hold my head high.

"Nope. You serve him. I'm going to serve this group of handsome men that have just walked in."

The local rugby team have just come in. They tend to mainly use the bar down the road, but tonight they've decided on a change. Lots and lots of fit men and because I look hot tonight, quite a few give me the patter, chatting me up and trying to hit on me.

"If looks could kill, tonight would be the end of the Waterthorpe Warriors," whispers Dan in my ear.

"I don't care," I answer.

"Well, the most amazing thing has been occurring all night. Every woman that has approached him has been turned away."

"Really?" I ask, still in the full flow of sarcasm.

"Really. He's pulled up a chair and is basically just staring at you."

"Well, I won't be staring back."

"Atta girl. Treat em mean to keep em keen."

"Dan, have you nothing better to do than give me a play by play account of dickhead's actions? Go and serve, we're busy."

"I'm the boss, so if I want to have fun winding up my staff, I say I can."

"You need to get laid yourself."

"Yeah, well, that's not going to happen anytime soon. My heart is still broken."

Dan had got divorced six months ago, and his head wasn't back in the game yet.

"Sorry, Dan. You'll get there." I pat his arm.

"Yes, well, until then, I'll live my life through you. So, did you shag him? What went wrong? Surely he didn't ask you to leave?"

"I got the full treatment. It's my fault. I did request it. I thought I might be different. Silly me. But I wasn't, so that's that."

"Sorry, Rach."

"Yeah, well, life goes on, and I have a whole rugby team to choose from."

I get back to serving, and one guy, in particular, hangs around the bar to talk to me.

When he goes off to the loo, I note from the corner of my eye that Evan jumps off his stool to follow him. Yes, maybe I had been looking, just a teeny bit. I can't help it if my eyes betray me.

A hand comes across my shoulders. "Stay here. I'll make sure no fists are thrown."

"Thanks, Dan."

Evan

She can give me the cold shoulder. I deserve it.

She can flirt with the Warriors if it makes her feel better. I deserve that too.

Her looking hot as fuck. Deserved.

But when she focuses on one particular player, one who I know has a worse reputation than I do, then it's hell, no. When he heads for the bathroom, I follow him in.

"Hey, Gary."

The guy looks at me like I'm a fanboy looking for some action.

"Hey, man. Sorry, I don't swing that way, if that's why you've followed me in. Feel free to have a good look while I take a slash though."

"Can you stop flirting with the barmaid. Only she's mine."

He takes his dick out of his pants. Jeez, it's bigger than mine. She's definitely not going there.

"She looks like a grown woman to me, and I ain't heard her say anything about a boyfriend. So, from where I stand, she's fair game."

I leap for him but ricochet backwards as my collar is grabbed.

"Out you go, Evan. Out of the loo and out of the pub until you can calm yourself down," says the landlord.

"I'm just looking out for Rachel."

"No, that's what I'm doing. So out you go. Rachel's fine. She's no intention of going home with this one. In fact, I've already said I'm driving her home tonight to make sure she gets back safe and sound, so there's no need for your theatrics."

Dan turns to Gary. "Sorry, mate. I'll leave you to piss in peace."

Then Dan grabs my shoulder and pushes me out of the bathroom. "Now, you can leave of your own accord, or I can make a great big show of throwing you out. Your choice."

I straighten my jacket. "I'll go home, all right. Just tell her, I've no intention of giving up."

"Well, I can tell you now, whatever you did last night you fucked up big time. You made her one of your many women, and I don't see how you're going to get back from that. I really don't."

I sigh. "I'll find a way, but tonight, I'll go home."

I walk out of the bar without a backward glance because if I see another of those blokes near Rachel, I'm going to murder someone.

Rachel

I watch as he walks out of the pub, half escorted by Dan.

Why do I feel sad he left? I should feel relieved.

I'm an idiot.

"What can I get you?" I ask the next customer.

Evan

'You made her one of your many women'. I did. It was what I wanted, wasn't it? To get her to leave me alone in case things didn't work out between us. But what have I achieved? I made things awkward and we never even gave it a go. I'm a damn idiot.

I go home and sink into the sofa, switching on a music channel. What can I do to show her she's different? An INXS video plays, and I get an idea. Looking at my watch, I see that it's quarter to ten. I just have time to pop to my local Sainsbury's and hope to God they sell white card and marker pens.

Rachel

Dan calls time and everyone groans because they want to carry on drinking. I'm more than ready for home. My brain needs a rest from thinking about Evan. I'm going to ask Dan if he'll let me out at the offy so I can buy myself some alcohol as I think that's the only way I'm going to get any sleep tonight.

And then Evan walks back in, clutching a load of A4 paper or card. Dan looks over at me, shaking his head. "Christ, I think Bob Dylan just walked in."

"Who?" I ask.

Dan's jaw drops. "Seriously? I think when this is all over you need a music lesson. Let's just say Bob sang about homesick blues while holding up cards and I think your bloke there's going to do the same."

"Oh, did he copy INXS? They did that."

"You don't know Bob Dylan, but you know INXS?" Dan shakes his head.

"Evan liked them, so I liked them," I admit.

"I'm going to turn the music off. I think it's time for the show. Second time in as many days you've had a bloke here for you. You'll be getting a reputation."

With the music switched off, Dan yells for people to drink up and leave, but everyone's waiting to see what Evan Hale, Womaniser, is doing standing in the doorway holding a load of paper.

He moves forward and comes closer to the bar, standing directly in front of me. "If you'll just hear me out, Rachel," he says, holding up his other hand. "If after this you don't want to know me, then I'll walk away, but please, let me do this."

"Okay." I nod.

So he holds up the cards, turning them around so that I can see the first one.

RACHEL SUMMERS

I WANTED YOU SINCE
YOU WERE FIFTEEN YEARS OLD

MY MUM TOLD ME
TO LEAVE YOU ALONE

SO, I DID

I WAS WRONG

BANNED

ALL THE OTHER WOMEN WERE
BECAUSE I COULDN'T HAVE YOU

THAT'S WHY THEY GOT
JUST ONE NIGHT

NO REPEATS

LAST NIGHT I WAS TRYING
TO LISTEN TO MY MOTHER'S
WARNING NOT TO HURT YOU

BUT I HURT YOU ANYWAY

I'M SORRY

I WAS WRONG

I WISH YOU WERE MY FIRST

I WISH I WAS YOUR FIRST

BUT WE CAN HAVE OTHER FIRSTS

BANNED

I WANT YOU TO HAVE MY OTHER
FIRSTS

ALL OF THEM

MY FIRST ALL NIGHTER WITH
A WOMAN

MY FIRST MAKE A WOMAN
BREAKFAST IN A MORNING

SCHMEXY FIRSTS I CAN'T WRITE
ABOUT.
YOU CAN HAVE THEM TOO.

YOU ALREADY HAVE ONE OF MY FIRSTS.

YOU'RE THE FIRST WOMAN
I'VE EVER LOVED
(OTHER THAN MY MUM).

I LOVE YOU
RACHEL SUMMERS.

I'M HERE IF YOU'LL HAVE ME.
TOTALLY ALL IN.

BE MY FIRST LIVE IN LOVER.

BANNED

BE MY WIFE.

HAVE MY CHILDREN.

MARRY ME
RACHEL SUMMERS.

Rachel

"What the fuck has she got that we haven't?" I hear a woman to the left of me say. "Two men in two fucking nights have proposed to her."

I drown out their words by climbing onto the bar, swinging over it and jumping onto Evan.

"Yes," I tell him. "If it all goes wrong, Evan, then it all goes wrong. No one can predict the future. Though proposing before a first date is a little strange."

"Oh, who makes all these bloody rules." He grabs my hand. "Come on, let's go break some, starting with the sleeping one, cos I'm knackered."

With a nod from Dan, I exit the pub with my Heavenly Evan.

THE END
(And they lived happily ever after.)

Want more Angel? Sign up to my newsletter here: www.subscribepage.com/AngelDevlin

ALL ABOUT ANGEL

I like writing short sexy stories that get readers hot under the collar while also entertaining and hopefully making the reader laugh.

Keep in contact with me here at

www.facebook.com/angeldevlinauthor

Find your favourite authors in one place!

www.subscribepage.com/bookhangoverlounge

Join us in the Book Hangover Lounge for giveaways

and goodies ... and the perfect place to recover from a long night with your latest book boyfriend!

Thank you!!!

ALSO BY ANGEL DEVLIN

geni.us/AngelDevlinAmazonPage

BANNED

LUCKED

HIS PERFECT MARTINI